Thinderella

Other *Young Puffin Read It Yourself* titles

HOGSEL AND GRUNTEL
Dick King-Smith and Liz Graham-Yooll

HUGE RED RIDING HOOD
Dick King-Smith and John Eastwood

THE JENIUS
Dick King-Smith and Peter Firmin

ROBIN HOOD AND HIS MISERABLE MEN
Dick King-Smith and John Eastwood

TRIFFIC
Dick King-Smith and Liz Graham-Yooll

DICK KING-SMITH

Thinderella

ILLUSTRATED BY
JOHN EASTWOOD

PUFFIN BOOKS

PUFFIN BOOKS

Published by the Penguin Group
Penguin Books Ltd, 27 Wrights Lane, London W8 5TZ, England
Penguin Putnam Inc., 375 Hudson Street, New York, New York 10014, USA
Penguin Books Australia Ltd, Ringwood, Victoria, Australia
Penguin Books Canada Ltd, 10 Alcorn Avenue, Toronto, Ontario, Canada M4V 3B2
Penguin Books (NZ) Ltd, Private Bag 102902, NSMC, Auckland, New Zealand

Penguin Books Ltd, Registered Offices: Harmondsworth, Middlesex, England

First published in *The Topsy-Turvy Storybook* by Victor Gollancz Ltd 1992
Published in Puffin Books 1998
5 7 9 10 8 6

Text copyright © Fox Busters Ltd, 1992
Illustrations copyright © John Eastwood, 1992, 1998
All rights reserved

The moral right of the author and illustrator has been asserted

Printed in Hong Kong by Wing King Tong

British Library Cataloguing in Publication Data
A CIP catalogue record for this book is available from the British Library

ISBN 0-141-30036-1

BEAR AND THE THREE GOLDILOCKS

There were once three sisters, triplets they were, as like as three peas in a pod, and all called Goldilocks.

This was partly because they all had golden hair, and partly because their mother was too stupid and lazy to choose different names for them so she called them Goldilocks One, Goldilocks Two and Goldilocks Three.

When the three Goldilocks grew up, they

left home and set up house together in a forest.

In the forest there lived a bear, called, quite simply, Bear.

One day the three Goldilocks left on a visit to their stupid lazy old mother, and while they were away, Bear came out of the trees and into their house.

Inside he found three identical beds, three identical chairs and three identical bowls of porridge.

Bear lay on the three beds in turn and smashed the lot.

Then he sat on the three chairs in turn and splintered the lot.

Then he tried the three bowls of porridge in turn and scoffed the lot.

Then he heard the three Goldilocks coming back, so, still feeling very hungry, he hid and listened.

"Look!" said Goldilocks One. "Someone's bust our beds!"

"Look!" said Goldilocks Two. "Someone's crushed our chairs!"

"Look!" said Goldilocks Three. "Someone's polished off our porridge!"

After that they never said another word,
ever again.

I expect you can guess why.
If not, I can't bear to tell you.

THERE WAS AN OLD WOMAN

There was an old woman who lived in a trainer,
She'd so many children, they drove her insaner.
She got a good price
For a few of the best,
And took seven pounds
Fifty pence
For the rest.

DING, DONG, BELL

Ding, dong, bell,
Johnny's in the well!
Who was it did that?
Our old pussy-cat.
Will she pull him out?
Never, though he shout.
What a clever cat she's been
To try to drown that Johnny Green,
Who always meant to do her harm
And teased and chased her round the farm.

THINDERELLA

Once upon a time there was a tall skinny girl named Thinderella.

Her arms were like sticks and her legs were like walking-sticks and an ordinary-sized dog-collar would have fitted round her middle with no trouble at all. She also had very big feet.

Thinderella had two older sisters called Gwendoline and Mirabelle, and they were as beautiful as she was plain. Handsome girls they were, with plenty of flesh on their bones, not fat but well-rounded. Buxom, you would have called them.

Gwendoline had long straight hair as black as a raven's wing, and Mirabelle had long curly hair as golden as ripe corn, and people called them the Lovely Sisters.

Thinderella's hair was short and mousy, and no one ever said anything nice about her.

"Scruffy thing!" they said. "And so scrawny too! It's hard to believe she's related to the Lovely Sisters. Why, she goes about in rags, and barefoot too!"

The reason for this was simple. Gwendoline and Mirabelle spent lavishly upon themselves, buying all manner of expensive clothes, but they did not even allow Thinderella pocket-money. Not that she had any pockets to put it in. All she got was the leftovers of food that the Lovely Sisters couldn't manage, just enough to give her the strength to do the cooking and the cleaning and the washing and the ironing and the mending.

One day a letter arrived addressed to the Misses Gwendoline and Mirabelle. It was an invitation to a Grand Ball, to celebrate the twenty-first birthday of Prince Hildebrand, the son of the King of that country.

"Look!" said Gwendoline, flourishing it under Thinderella's pinched little nose.

"But don't touch!" said Mirabelle. "Your hands are filthy."

"I've been doing the fires," said Thinderella.

"Well, go and wash," said Gwendoline.

"And then you can help us on with our best clothes," said Mirabelle. "So that we can go downtown."

"And buy some even better ones for the Ball."

When the great night came, and the Lovely Sisters had set off for the Ball, sumptuously dressed and glittering with jewellery, Thinderella sat by the kitchen fire, staring sadly at the glowing embers.

"How I wish I could go to the Ball," she whispered softly, and two big tears ran down her grimy cheeks.

"So you shall!" said a voice.

Thinderella looked round to see a strange little man sitting cross-legged on the kitchen table. He had very long hair and a big moustache and a bushy beard, so that all Thinderella could see of his face was a red nose and a pair of twinkling eyes.

"Who are you?" she said.

"I," said the little man, "am

your Hairy Godfather, and you *shall* go to the
Ball. Run off and have a good wash, Thinders,
and put some clean clothes on."

"But I haven't any," said Thinderella.

"You'll be surprised," said the Hairy
Godfather, and sure enough when she reached
her dark attic room, there was a ball-gown laid
out ready on the bed.

Quickly Thinderella washed herself,
especially her feet which were very big and flat
through always going about barefoot, and she
put on the gown. But, she thought, I have no
shoes, and then she looked under the bed and

there was a pair of very large slippers, made
all of glass. And she tried them on and they
fitted perfectly.

Hastily Thinderella combed her short
mousy hair with her newly-cleaned fingers
and went downstairs again.

"Not bad," said her Hairy Godfather. "The gown's a bit plain, but it'll do."

"But please," said Thinderella, "I'm a bit plain too. Prince Hildebrand is sure to dance the night away with Gwendoline and Mirabelle but he'll never look twice at me."

"You'll be surprised," said the Hairy Godfather. "Now then, got a pumpkin about the place?"

"No."

"Got any mice?"

"Mice? What for?"

"Oh forget it," said the Hairy Godfather. "It won't take you long to walk. It's not far and it isn't raining. Have a good time. Oh, and by the way, don't stay there after midnight."

In fact, walking even a short distance in glass slippers is murder on the feet, and by the time Thinderella arrived at the Palace, hers were agony. She hobbled into the ballroom and flopped down on a chair and stuck her thin legs out and wriggled her toes inside the glass slippers.

At that moment a young man who was walking by fell over her enormous great feet.

"Oh sorry!" gasped Thinderella.

"My fault," said the young man. "I wasn't

16

looking where I was going," and indeed
Thinderella could see that he wore very thick
spectacles.

"By the way," he said, "my name's
Hildebrand," and he stuck out a hand, vaguely
in her direction.

"Oh!" she said. The Prince, she thought.
He's not very handsome and he's *very* short-
sighted, but he's got ever such a nice smile.

"Happy birthday," she said.

"Oh, thanks a lot," said the Prince.

She's got ever such a nice voice, he thought.

"I won't ask you to dance," he said. "I'm so clumsy, I'm always treading on people's feet."

"You would on mine," said Thinderella. "They're huge," and she took off one glass slipper and gave it to him.

"Have a look at that," she said.

Just then Gwendoline and Mirabelle came by in all their finery, and their lovely eyes positively bulged at the sight of their sister neatly dressed and talking to the Prince. But before they could open their lovely mouths, the clock began to strike.

"Oh gosh!" cried Thinderella. "Midnight!" And she dashed away, leaving Prince Hildebrand holding one of the glass slippers.

In fact the clock was only striking ten, and when she got home, her Hairy Godfather was still sitting on the kitchen table, eating pickled gherkins.

"Hello, Thinders," he said. "You're early. What happened? Didn't the Prince look twice at you?"

"Oh more than that," said Thinderella. "He's very short-sighted, you see. But he's ever so nice, Hairy Godfather. I'm so glad I went to the Ball."

"Good," said the Hairy Godfather. "And goodnight," and he disappeared.

When Thinderella woke up next morning the ball-gown and the remaining glass slipper had disappeared too, so she got up to do the housework in her usual ragged clothes. She made breakfast for the Lovely Sisters and took it up to them.

They were furious with her.

"What were you doing at the Ball?" shouted Gwendoline.

"And where did you get that gown?" yelled Mirabelle.

"And what d'you think you were doing chatting up the Prince?" they both screamed.

At that moment there was a knock at the front door.

Thinderella ran down and opened it and there stood Prince Hildebrand, holding the other glass slipper and peering at her with his weak eyes through his thick spectacles.

"Is there anyone here whose foot will fit this slipper?" he said, coming in and tripping over the mat. "If so, I will marry her."

The Lovely Sisters, who had been leaning over the banisters listening, came rushing down the stairs crying "It's mine! It's mine!" but of course when they tried it on in turn, it was far too big for their lovely little feet.

But when Thinderella put her great beetle-crusher in the slipper, it fitted perfectly!

"I told you," she said to the Prince. "They're huge. Don't you remember?"

How could I forget that nice voice, thought Prince Hildebrand, and he smiled his nice smile and put out his hand, vaguely in Thinderella's direction.

"I'm offering you this hand in marriage," he said. "Will you take it?"

And Thinderella took it, while the Lovely Sisters hurried away, their lovely faces contorted with jealous rage. So angry were they that they did not notice a little man with very long hair and a big moustache and a bushy beard, sitting cross-legged under the staircase, and grinning all over his face, or as much of it as could be seen.

The short-sighted Prince of course did not notice either, but Thinderella saw him and they winked at one another.

"By the way," said Prince Hildebrand as his betrothed helped him down the front steps, "I don't even know your name!"

"It's Thinderella," said Thinderella.

"What a perfectly beautiful name," said the Prince, blinking at her through his thick spectacles, "for a perfectly beautiful girl."

LITTLE MISS MUFFET

A whopping great spider
With four flies inside her
Was eating a fifth on a tuffet,
When suddenly coshed
And disgustingly squashed
By a fat little girl called Miss Muffet.

RAPUNZEL

There was once a particularly silly girl by the ridiculous name of Rapunzel.

So stupid was Rapunzel that she allowed a witch to imprison her in the top of a tall tower that had neither door nor stairway, but only a little window at the top.

Now Rapunzel had lovely blonde hair which grew so long that there was no room for all of it in the top of the tower. So she hung it out of the window, all twenty yards of it, and the witch climbed up it each time she visited Rapunzel.

That hurt, of course – it would, wouldn't it? – and one day stupid Rapunzel said to herself, "If I cut my hair short, then the witch wouldn't be able to hurt me by climbing up it." (It didn't occur to her that in that case she would have nothing to eat, since the witch only climbed up in order to bring her food.)

Anyway, the next time she felt the witch climbing up, she took a pair of scissors and cut off her hair close to her head.

What stupid Rapunzel didn't know was that it wasn't the witch who was climbing up. It was a handsome prince, attracted by the sight of twenty yards of lovely blonde hair and wanting to see who was at the other end of it, and he was half-way up just as the hair was cut off.

Down he fell, wallop, and before he could get up again Rapunzel, who was leaning out of the window to see what had happened, leaned too far.

Down she fell, crash, right on top of the prince, and I can tell you that it was hate at first sight.

As for the witch, she fell about laughing.

THE QUEEN OF HEARTS

The Queen of Hearts
She made some tarts,
All jammy, fresh and hot.
The Knave of Hearts
He stole those tarts
And scoffed the blooming lot.
"How very mean,"
Remarked the Queen,
And vowed no more to bake.
As for the Knave,
His feasting gave
Him dreadful tummy-ache.

LITTLE BO-PEEP

Little Bo-Peep
Has lost her sheep.
She's terribly down on her luck,
And well might she cry
For the rustlers came by
And drove them away in a truck.

THE WOLF AND THE SEVEN LITTLE KIDS

Every mother knows that it's quite wrong to go out of the house and leave her kids unattended. But there was once a nanny-goat foolish enough to do just that.

Off she went, leaving her seven kids behind. What's more, she must have known there was a wolf about, because she warned them not to open the door.

But when she returned, she found that the wolf had indeed called at her house. He'd fooled the kids into letting him in and then he'd scoffed the lot. Except one, the smallest, who'd hidden inside the grandfather clock.

Well now, this dumb nanny-goat had a really nutty idea. "Get some scissors and a needle and thread," she said to the smallest kid.

"Why, Mum?" said the smallest kid.

"It's simple," said the nanny-goat. "We'll find the wolf asleep. We'll cut him open and out will pop your six brothers and sisters. Then we'll fill his belly up with stones and sew him up again."

"Why, Mum?" said the smallest kid.

"Use your brains," said his mother. "When the wolf wakes up, he'll be thirsty, and he'll go to the river and topple in and drown."

"Why, Mum?" said the smallest kid.

"Because of the weight of the stones inside him, of course."

The nanny-goat was right about the first bit. They did find the wolf asleep.

But (as you might expect) the very first touch of the point of the scissors on his stomach woke him up sharply.

He swallowed the smallest kid in one gulp.

Then he said to the nanny-goat, "I should have thought you would have known that it's quite wrong to go out of the house and leave your kids unattended?"

"I do! I do!" bleated the nanny-goat. "I'll never do it again as long as I live!"

"Which is no time at all," said the wolf, licking his chops.

GEORGIE PORGIE

Georgie Porgie, sloppy and sly,
Kissed the girls and made them cry;
But when all the boys came out,
It was Georgie's turn to shout.

HICKORY, DICKORY, DOCK

Hickory, dickory, dock,
The mouse got in the clock;
The unfortunate thing
Became caught in the spring,
Squishery, squashery, shplock!

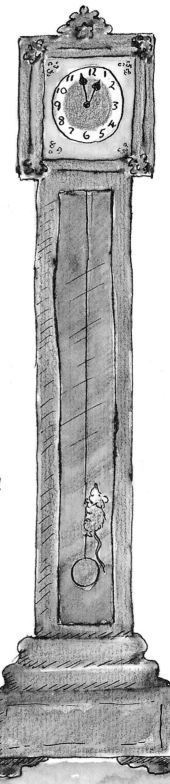